For Uncle Albert
S.P.

For Viggo
C.J.

ORCHARD BOOKS
338 Euston Road, London NW1 3BH
*Orchard Books Australia*
Level 17/207 Kent Street, Sydney, NSW 2000

This text was first published in the form of a gift collection called
*The Sleeping Princess* by Orchard Books in 2002

This edition first published in hardback in 2012
First paperback publication in 2013

ISBN 978 1 40830 841 7 (hardback)
ISBN 978 1 40830 842 4 (paperback)

Text © Saviour Pirotta 2002
Illustrations © Cecilia Johansson 2012

The rights of Saviour Pirotta to be identified as the author and
Cecilia Johansson to be identified as the illustrator of this work
have been asserted by them in accordance
with the Copyright, Designs and Patents Act, 1988.

A CIP catalogue record for this book is available
from the British Library.

1 3 5 7 9 10 8 6 4 2 (hardback)
1 3 5 7 9 10 8 6 4 2 (paperback)

Printed in China

Orchard Books is a division of Hachette Children's Books,
an Hachette UK company.
www.hachette.co.uk

# Grimm's Fairy Tales
## Rumpelstiltskin

Written by Saviour Pirotta
Illustrated by Cecilia Johansson

ORCHARD

Once there was a poor miller who had
a beautiful daughter. He lived in a mill,
on the edge of a wood where the king
often went hunting.

"My daughter is so clever," he boasted to the king one day. "She can spin ordinary straw into gold."

The king loved gold more than anything.
"Send your daughter to my palace," he said
to the miller, "and we'll see if she can."

The next morning, when the miller's daughter arrived at the palace, the king showed her into a little chamber. He pointed to a big pile of straw and a spinning wheel.

"Spin this into gold by the morning,"
he said, "or I'll have you put to death."
Then the king locked and bolted the door.

The girl started to cry, for she had no way
of turning the straw to gold. Suddenly
the locked door opened and
a goblin came leaping in.

"What will you give me if I spin the straw
into gold for you?" he asked.

"My necklace," said the girl.

"Your necklace will do nicely," said the goblin.

He sat down at the wheel and started spinning. In no time at all, the straw had been spun into pure gold.

The goblin took the
girl's necklace and quickly
left the room.

At daybreak, the king unlocked the door.
When he saw the reels of gold, he clapped his
hands and servants brought in a pile
of straw twice as big as the first one.

"Spin that into gold or
you'll lose your head," he
said again. And he locked
and bolted the door once more.

The girl started weeping again. But no sooner had the sun set than the goblin appeared again.

"What will you give me if I spin your straw into gold once more?" he asked.

"I'll give you my ring," answered the girl.

"Your ring will do nicely," said the goblin.
He took his place on the stool and the straw
was soon a glittering heap of gold.

The king couldn't believe his eyes when he
opened the door again at the crack of dawn.

He locked the girl in a room where there was a pile of straw THREE times the size of the first one.

At night, the goblin appeared and offered to help the girl again.

"But I have nothing left to give you," she said.

"Then promise to give me your first child when you have it," said the goblin.

The girl was so desperate, she promised the goblin her first baby.

The goblin sat at the stool. Once more the spinning wheel turned – *whirr, whirr, whirr* . . .

. . . and before sunrise the straw had been spun into shimmering gold.

In the morning, the king took the beautiful miller's daughter as his bride.

Time passed, and the new queen had a
baby. She was so happy, she forgot all about
the little goblin who had helped her.

But one night, the little man appeared, grinning slyly from ear to ear.

"It's time you gave me what you promised," he said.

The young queen clasped the baby to her chest. "I will give you anything you ask for," she told the goblin, "but please don't take away my child."

"I am an honest man," said the goblin, "so I shall give you three days' grace."

"If you guess my name correctly, I shall let you keep the child."

The queen lay awake all night, trying to remember all the names she had ever heard.
Meanwhile, she sent out a messenger to track down all the unusual names he could find.

When the goblin arrived the next morning, the queen started with the names she knew: Alex, Peter, John ... But the goblin just shook his head at each and every one of them.

On the second day the queen repeated all the strange names she had read in the king's library: Loftus, Pimpernel, Fenugreek ...

But once again the goblin shook his head.

On the third day, the messenger returned
with news. "Your Highness," he said, "I have
not been able to find a new name in two
days. But early this morning I came across
a little house with a log fire outside.

"Dancing on one foot was a curious goblin like the one you described. He was singing:

'Today I bake, tomorrow brew,
Merrily I dance and sing,
For the queen will never find out
My name is RUMPELSTILTSKIN.'"

When the queen heard the name, she started
singing and dancing herself.

As soon as the goblin arrived, she ushered him straight into her chamber. "Is your name Tom?" she said.

"I'm afraid that's not my name," answered the goblin.

"Then could it be Hamish?" asked the queen.

"I'm afraid it's not Hamish either," said the goblin.

"Well then," said the queen, "is it RUMPELSTILTSKIN?"

The goblin was furious. "How did you find that out?" he roared. He stamped his foot so hard it went right through the floor.

He tried in vain to pull it out. In the end he pulled so hard, he tore himself in two and died.

So the poor miller's daughter who had become queen, lived happily ever after with her king and her child.

Nimmo, James E.; and Combs, Dan, 110
Nobel prize, 93, 117 n. 10, 218
noise, 11, 167, 178
noogenetic processes, 162, 163, 169, 173, 177
Nora, Simon; and Minc, Alain, 195
North American Telegraph Company, 189
Northern Electric, 193
Northern Telecom. *See* Northern Electric
Northern Telephone Company, 191
Nova Scotia, 196 n. 7
*Novum Organum* (Bacon), 77, 78

objectification, 101
objectivity, 168
Office of Radio Research, 40
Olewiler, Nancy, 95, 118 n. 17
Ontario, 186, 197 n. 11
Ontario Telephone Service Commission, 197 n. 12
optimality, 26, 27
organic, 178
organic conception of knowledge, 168
organic conception of society, 65, 104, 218
organization, 42, 45, 131, 136, 160, 166, 171, 215, 222, 223
organizational revolution, 170
*Ottawa Citizen*, 111
*Our Common Future*, 87, 119 n. 21
ownership. *See* property
Oxford University, 159, 213
ozone, 87

Palmer Margaret, 121 n. 38
Parenti, Michael, 121 n. 39
Park, Robert, 65, 80, 159
Parker, Ian, 29, 138 n. 5, 178 n. 12, 178 n. 15, 207
patent, 188, 189, 193, 195
pay TV, 200, 217
Peirce, C.S., 23, 24, 48 n. 8, 143, 145, 148, 155 n. 7
Pelton, Joseph, 30
Penetrative Powers of the Price System, 22, 218

perception, 167, 168, 174, 178 n. 12
perfect competition, 62, 77
perfect knowledge, 92
Perinbanayagam, R.S., 21–26, 43, 44, 48 n. 8
persona ficta, 223
persuasion, 24, 56, 58, 61
Peterson, Theodore, 111
Pigou, A.C., 90, 91, 94, 95, 98, 116 n. 6, 117 n. 8
*Phenomenon of Man* (Teilhard de Chardin),177
phenotype, 160–164
Philippines, 113
Phillips, Bruce, 204
Pittsburgh, 192
*Place of Science in Modern Civilization, The* (Veblen), 155 158
Ploman, Edward, 19 n. 8, 37
Polanyi, Karl, 100, 120 n. 26
political economy, 2, 4, 5, 24, 28, 40, 43–46, 51, 52, 61–65, 69–85, 89, 141, 184, 225
classical, 127
defined, 70–71
types of, 71
pollution, 87, 94, 95, 117 n. 12, 118 n. 17, 119 n. 22
poor vs rich. *See* rich vs poor
Popper, Karl, 79
population 73, 127ff, 163–164, 177. *See also* checks
Population Principle (Malthus), 5, 128–134, 162, 175
Porat, Marc, 9, 22, 29, 30, 47 n. 2, 79
positivism, 58, 66 n. 1
Posner, Richard, 27, 28
post–civilization, 173–174
post–industrial society, 1
post modernism, 1
Postal Telegraph Company, 187, 188
Potvin, Rose, 213
power, 40, 51, 64, 65, 71–75, 77, 144, 184, 226
power relations, 6, 59
powerplays, 192, 195, 202–204
poverty, 87, 88, 116 n. 2
pragmatism, 1 143
Prang, Margaret, 214
praxis, 70
predation, 186, 188–190
preferences, 3, 14, 16, 92, 97

and knowledge, 11, 105, 165
and money, 2, 3, 10–11
and organization, 45, 176, 215
and theory of the firm, 33
and transnationals, 202–204
and uncertainty, 22, 24, 33–34, 47 n. 5
as agent of change, 126
as commodity, 3, 4, 15–17, 28, 30, 44, 219
as evolutionary agent, 176
as factor of production, 3, 4, 15–17, 89, 103–106
as final output, 3, 15
as form, 4, 41–42
as gift, 4, 44
as negentropy, 4, 89, 102–103, 105, 120 n. 31, 176, 215
as power, 18, 40, 89
defined,11, 41–43, 120, n. 30, 121 n. 33
industries, 3
measurability of, 4, 16, 39
non quantifiability of, 4, 16
prices as, 2, 60, 91–100
processing of, 5
production of, 2, 10
properties of, 12–13, 15–17, 31, 36, 37, 40, 43, 105, 205, 223–224
types of, 45
units of, 11, 38
*See also* mathematical theory of information
information commodity, 3, 6, 9, 16, 19, 29, 30, 36–39, 205–207, 218
information economics, 3, 22–24, 26, 28, 32–36
information economy, 3, 22, 28–30, 115
Information Highway, 5–6, 46, 96, 113, 182, 191, 194, 199–210, 217
Information Highway Advisory Council, 200
information industries, 3, 10, 15, 62, 109–112
information processors, 106
*Information Revolution and Its Implications for Canada* (Serafini and Andrieu), 182
information workers, 1, 9, 29, 33
Ingrao Bruna; and Israel, Giorgio 30
Innis, Harold, 22, 40, 60, 75, 82, 113, 121 n. 40, 152, 154 n. 2, 169, 187, 212, 218
Inns, G. D., 197 n. 11

*Instant World*, 183
instinct, 144, 147, 155 n. 7, 175
Institutionalism, 52, 63, 64, 72, 75–76, 80, 81, 135, 143–145, 153–154,
institutions, 5, 64, 75, 131, 141, 143–145, 153, 154, 175
intellectual property, 1, 6, 9, 45, 207
internal validity, 28, 38–40, 44
interpretation, 145, 148
interpretent, 23–26, 48 n. 8
invisible hand, 55, 62, 74, 76, 80, 107
Irwin, Manley, 82, 196
ISDN, 199, 200

Jacob, François, 125
James, William, 143, 224–225
Jenner, R. A., 38
Jevons, Stanley, 69
Jonscher, Charles, 22, 32, 34, 35
*Journals of the House of Commons*, 196 n. 8
justice. *See* fairness

Kaplan, Abraham, 30
Kapp, William, 119 n. 23
Katz, E., 66 n. 6
KDKA, 192, 193
Kenora, Ontario, 191
Kern, Stephen, 192
Keynes, John Maynard, 139 n. 10
Klamer, A., 24, 43, 63, 70
Klapp, Orin, 11
Knight, Frank, 27, 33, 47 n. 6, 63, 159
knowledge, 11, 77, 105, 106, 130, 136, 143, 145, 147, 148–149, 153, 160, 163, 166–168, 171, 172, 176
knowledge structures, 106–107, 144–145, 161, 164–168, 172
knowledge workers, 29
Koestler, Arthur, 79, 116 n. 3, 139 n. 12
Kristofferson, Kris, 122 n. 42
Kroker, Arthur, 181
Kuhn, Thomas, 19 n. 2, 43, 67 n. 8, 106, 125, 151

labor, 3–6, 15, 82, 89, 98, 130, 204
commoditization of, 74
division of, 113 138 n. 5, 206–208

Lamarck, Jean Baptiste, 161, 176 n. 3
Lamberton, D., 22
land, 3, 88, 89, 98, 100, 101, 120 n. 24, 120 n. 26, 130, 131
language, 42, 43, 165, 219
Lasswell, Harold, 57
Laurier, Wilfred, 190
law of arithmetic food increase, 175
law of conservation, 102, 104, 171, 172, 176
law of diminishing growth, 162, 177 n. 7
law of diminishing returns, 131, 134, 138 n. 8, 177 n. 7
law of minimal effects, 66 n. 6, 67 n. 7
law of survival of the fittest, 134
Lazarsfeld, Paul Felix, 65 n. 1, 66 n. 6, 67 n. 7
League for Social Reconstruction, 214
learning, 166
Lears, T. Jackson, 110
legal liability, 91
legal system, 52, 71, 81
Lerner, Daniel, 17
Lerner, Max, 142
Leshan, L.; and Margenau, H., 10
Lewis, C. S., 142
liberalism, 72–74, 81, 82, 110
licences, 118 n. 17, 188, 193
limits, 99
Lippmann, Walter, 18, 51, 82, 151
Litman, Barry, 31
local exchange, 191
long distance, 189, 191, 209 n. 1
love, 45, 115, 170–171
Lowery, S.; and de Fleur, M., 39, 59
Lucács, Georg, 66 n. 3, 84 n. 7
Luckman, Thomas, 17
Lurie, Alison, 60
Lusseyran, Jacques, 222
Lutz, Mark A.; and Lux, Kenneth, 47 n. 1
Lux, Kenneth, 71, 72, 77, 81, 114

Macbeth, Norman, 79
MacGibbon, D. A., 187
Machine. *See* Technology
Machlup, Fritz, 11, 22, 28, 30, 33
Macpherson, C. B., 117 n. 12, 201
Magder, Ted, 64

mainstream economics. *See* neoclassical economics
Maisonrouge, Jacques, 112, 202, 204
Malaysia, 113
Malthus, Thomas Robert, 5, 69, 73, 74, 76, 79, 83, 125–140, 138 n. 5, 138 n. 6, 138 n. 7, 139 n. 10, 139 n. 11, 142, 160, 175–176, 225
Mammon, 152
*Manitoba Free Press*, 213
Manitoba Government Telephones, 190
Manley, John, 200
Maquiladoras, 113, 209 n. 4
Marcel, Gabriel, 69, 121 n. 37
March of Time. *See* Evolution
Marconi Wireless, 193, 197
marginal analysis, 14, 15
marginalization, 1
Market, 4, 41, 51, 54, 55, 59, 61, 71, 72, 74, 76–81, 91–94, 126
market failure, 61, 62
markets, 1, 22, 30, 32, 63, 81, 91–94
Marshall, Alfred, 19 n. 1, 32, 33, 69, 70, 89, 90, 137 n. 3, 139 n. 10
Marshallian partial analysis, 31
Marx, Karl, 69, 74, 83, 84 n. 5, 100, 120 n. 25, 138 n. 7, 151, 152, 157 n. 21
Marxism, 52, 72, 74–75, 81, 82
Massey Commission, 194
material realm, 52, 64, 224
materialism, 83, 160
mathematical theory of communication, 12–14, 38, 47 n. 7, 57, 59, 66 n. 6, 120 n. 31, 121 n. 33, 177
Mattelart, A., 201
matter, 10–11, 14, 41–42, 89, 102, 104, 105, 171, 176, 224
Mayor, Frederico, 209
maximization principle, 53
McCloskey, Donald, 9, 44
McCracken, Grant, 25, 26, 60
McLuhan Marshall, 2, 9, 60, 152, 166, 212, 222
Meade, G.H., 25
Meadows, Donella, 107, 112
meaning, 143, 145, 165, 166
measurement, 30, 32, 35, 42
media, 163, 169–170, 203, 216
  *See also* information industries
medicare, 212, 214, 219
medium of transmission, 41

Meek, Ronald, 130
Meeker–Lowry, Susan, 113, 209 n. 4
Megarry, Roy, 109, 110
Melody, William, 113, 201, 202
Menger, Karl, 69
methodological collectivism, 2, 43, 63, 141, 154, 219
methodological individualism, 26, 43, 53–55, 58, 59, 63, 66 n. 1, 96, 131, 134, 136, 137, 138 n. 3, 140 n. 13, 141, 218
Mexico, 113, 208, 209 n. 4
microeconomics. *See* neoclassical economics
Mill, J. S., 69, 70, 73
Miller, Daniel, 25, 26
Milton, John, 17
minimum wage laws, 113
Mishan, E., 90, 116 n. 5, 118 n. 16
Mitchell Wesley, 19 n. 1, 64, 66 n. 2, 69, 72, 73, 75, 83 n. 1, 128
models, 70, 77, 127
monetarization. *See* commoditization
*Monetary Times*, 186
money, 2, 3, 10, 14, 21, 30, 32, 65, 98, 153, 189, 218–219
monopoly, 34, 55, 186
Montreal, 192, 193, 196 n. 4
*Montreal Daily Star*, 192
Montreal Telegraph Company, 186, 188
moral philosophy, 4, 76
Morris, Charles, 66 n. 6
Mosco, Vincent, 31; and Wasko, Janet, 62
Mowlana, Hamid; Gerbner, George; and Schiller, Herbert I., 217
Mulgan, G., 201
Mumford, Lewis, 152
Murchie, Guy, 223
Musgrave, Richard, 17
music, 194
myths, 4, 72, 75–80, 125, 137 n. 1, 181–184

naming, 98–99
NAFTA, 113
nation states, 6
National Bell, 188
national sovereignty, 112, 113, 202, 207
natural law, 133, 134

natural monopoly, 183, 184, 1[
natural rights, 134
Natural Selection, 79, 80, 84 n. 127, 132–135, 155 n. 5
Nature, 88, 115, 132
*Nature of Things*, 111
negentropy, 4, 89, 102–103, 120
Nelkin, Dorothy, 79
Nelson, Joyce, 113, 116 n. 2, 12[
Nelson, P., 36
neoclassical economics, 1, 3, 10[ 51–65, 69, 70, 107, 114–115, 2[ 225, 226
  and break–down in commun[
  and environmental degradat[ 6, 91–100
  and evolution, 137 n. 3
  and fairness, 71
  and information/communica[ 2, 6, 14, 88, 141, 176
  and labor/capital, 6
  and media, 52
  and methodological individu[ 53–54, 134, 141
  and power, 71
  and prices, 2, 3
  and rich/poor, 6
  as ideology, 63
  as psychic balm, 61
  constancy of tastes, 55
  infusion with communicatory siderations, 6
  models, 77
  treatment of commodities, 61–[
neoconservativism, 2, 6, 73, 74, 8[ 134, 202, 218–20
neo–Darwinism. *See* neoconserva[ ism
Nevitt, Barrington, 40, 223
*New Atlantis* (Bacon), 7
*New Commonwealth*, 214
New Brunswick, 197 n. 7
New World Information and Com[ nication Order (NWICO), 18, 44, n. 5
New World Order, 6, 96, 205, 220
New York, 193
*New York Times*, 210
newspapers, 185
niche, 163–164, 173, 177 n. 7
Nichols, M. E., 185, 196 n. 4
nihilism, 142

constant in neoclassicism, 55, 62, 106
Preston, William; Herman, Edward S.;
    and Schiller, Herbert I., 44, 207
price search, 35–36
price system, 10, 22, 32–33, 73, 99, 164
prices, 2, 10–11, 15, 16, 30, 32, 35, 60, 62,
    65, 88, 89, 93, 96–100, 101, 114
Prince Edward Island, 196 n. 7
*Principles of Economics* (Marshall), 69,
    89
*Principles of Political Economy* (Mill), 70
print, 169
Privacy Commissioner, 204
privatization, 6, 28, 119 n. 19, 202, 218
probability. *See* chance
production, 3, 4, 5, 14, 89, 103, 106, 143,
    154, 160–164, 171, 174
production posibilities curve, 98
profit, 33, 34, 101, 138 n. 3
progress, 74, 76, 79, 135
*Progress and Poverty* (George), 120 n. 27
propaganda, 75, 110, 121 n. 37
property, 63, 74, 75, 81, 112, 131, 133,
    147, 149, 152, 156 n. 14, 157 n. 17, 157
    n. 18, 157 n. 19, 186, 195, 222
*Protestant Ethic and the Theory of Capi-
    talism, The* (Weber), 225
psychology. *See* human nature
public broadcasting, 194, 205, 211, 214,
    215
public goods, 17, 205
public philosophy, 82
public services, 6, 184
publishing, 185–186, 195
pure competition, 56

quantification, 4, 13, 32, 34, 37–39
Quebec, 186

Radner, Roy, 36
radio, 170, 193–194, 213
railways, 186, 187
Ramstad, Yngve, 64, 153
rate rebalancing, 191
RCA, 193
reductionism, 27, 127
*Regina Manifesto*, 214
reification, 74, 76, 84 n. 7
    of market, 55

religion, 78, 83, 142, 224–225
resale and sharing, 191
resources, 4, 94, 174, 204, 207
    depletion of, 88, 130
Review of Regulatory Framework
    (CRTC), 191, 200
Reynolds Lloyd, 154
Ricardo, David, 69, 73, 74, 98, 137 n. 2
rich vs poor, 2, 46, 74, 97, 119 n. 23, 130,
    131, 133, 201–206, 217, 219, 221
Riesman, David, 154 n. 2
Rifkin, J., 38
Righter, R., 17
rights of way, 189, 190
risk, 33
Ritchie, L. David, 38, 120 n. 31
Roach, Collen, 210
Robins, Kevin; and Webster, Frank, 63
Robinson, Gertrude, 65
Rogers Communications, 188
Roper, Elmo, 58
Roszak, Theodore, 18
Rothchild, Michael, 35, 36
Rotstein, Abraham, 62, 66 n. 5
Royal Commission on National Devel-
    opment (Massey), 193
Royal Society of Canada, 215
Ruben, Brent, 116 n. 3
Rousseau, J.J., 84 n. 4
Rubin Michael, 29
Ruth, Matthias, 102, 103
Rutherford, Paul, 185

sacredness, 99
Samuels, Warren J., 21, 24, 43, 61, 63,
    65, 75, 117 n. 6, 153
Samuelson, Paul, 16, 71
Saskatchewan, 214
Saskatchewan Government Tele-
    phones, 190
satellites, 170, 194, 217
savagery, 147–148, 152, 156 n. 15
Say's Law, 225
Schiller, Herbert I., 24, 44, 82, 110, 121
    n. 39, 202, 221
Schramm, Wilbur, 57, 66
Schumacher, E. F., 114, 206
Schumpeter, Joseph, 45, 47 n. 6, 82, 159
science, 77, 78, 130, 148, 153, 156 n. 10,
    168, 178

Scitovsky, Tibor, 24, 61

Scott, Frank, 214

selection, 5, 132, 142, 153, 161, 168. *See also* Natural Selection

self–love. *See* greed

Seligman, Ben, 34

semiology. *See* semiotics

semiosis, 23
  defined, 48 n. 8, 143

semiotics, 21, 155 n. 7

sensory stimuli, 106, 166

Serafini, S.; and Andrieu, M., 22, 182

Serafy, Salah El, 48 n. 11

Shannon and Weaver. *See* mathematical theory of communication

Shaw, George Bernard, 139 n. 10

Shepherd, William, 31

signals, 167–168, 178

signification, 165

signs, 12, 23–25, 43, 165, 169

Single Integrated Network (SIN), 199, 200

Skinner, B. F., 221

*Small Is Beautiful* (Schumacher),114

Smith Adam, 4, 53, 55, 56, 61, 66 n. 2, 69, 72, 74, 76, 78, 83, 83 n. 1, 114, 115, 137 n. 2, 138 n. 5, 222

Smith, Anthony, 17, 202

Smythe, Dallas, 66 n.1, 109, 212

social construction, 1, 141, 151, 152, 167–168

Social Darwinism, 5, 79, 127, 131–134, 136, 139 n. 11, 142, 154, 154 n. 2, 201

*Social Planning for Canada*, 214

social policy, 6, 119 n. 19, 133, 134, 140 n. 13, 154, 203, 207, 208,218, 224,

social species.*See* artifact

socialism, 142, 154 n. 3

socialists, 134

Society for General Systems Research, 159

sociology of knowledge. *See* social construction

Solomon, Jack, 43

Solow, Robert, 44, 87, 98, 105, 118 n. 15

sound recordings, 169–170

space, 202, 217

spaceship earth, 174

Special Joint Committee (Foreign Policy), 202–204, 208

specialization, 137 n. 3

Spence, Michael, 22, 36, 37, 39

Spencer, Herbert, 4, 65, 76, 79, 83, 85 n. 12, 125, 133–134, 137 n. 3, 147, 154

Spry, Graham, 2, 6, 211–220

Spry, Irene, 212

Sri Lanka, 113

standardization, 151

Staniland, M., 84 n. 3

Stanton, Frank, 58

starvation, 131, 133

static analysis, 26, 47 n. 4, 96, 106–7, 127, 143, 176

stationary state, 131

Stentor Telecom Policy Inc, 182, 188, 199, 209 n. 3

Steuart, James, 138 n. 5

Stigler, George, 15, 22, 27, 28, 31, 34–36, 55, 56, 62, 66 n. 6, 67 n. 8, 71, 74, 93, 106, 117 n. 9, 218

Stiglitz, Joseph, 22, 33, 36, 37, 39, 98, 105, 118 n. 15

stimulus, 147

structure. *See* organization

struggle, 133–134, 136, 138 n. 7, 153, 175

St. Thomas (Ontario), 212

subsidies, 95, 98, 18 n. 17, 119 n. 20, 209 n. 1

substitutability, 1, 98, 99, 101, 115

subsystem, 88, 104

Sumner, William Graham, 133–134, 142, 154 n. 2, 225

superculture. *See* globalization

supply, 3, 14, 16, 35, 41, 126

survival, 132, 144, 153

sustainable development, 48 n. 11, 89, 108, 116, 116 n. 4, 208

Suzuki, David, 46, 109, 110, 111, 116, 121 n. 38, 202

symbolic interaction, 21, 2327, 48 n. 8

symbolic realm, 52, 64, 223

symbolization, 46, 63

symbols, 169

system, 5, 57, 88, 101–107, 116 n. 3, 120 n. 28, 120 n. 29 ,153, 159, 221–223

tax, 98, 118 n. 17, 118 n. 19, 119 n. 20, 204, 207

Team Canada, 203, 207, 208

technique, 184

technological change, 1

technological dependence, 5, 181
technological determinism, 5, 151, 181, 183–184
Technological Evolution, 80, 181, 183, 216–217
technological imperative, 5, 181–184, 192, 195
Technology, 4, 5, 72, 76–81, 84 n. 11, 181–184, 195, 195 n. 1, 203
Tehranian, Majid, 114
Teilhard de Chardin, Pierre, 177
telecommunication, 112–114, 199–210
telecommuting, 205
telegraph, 185–189, 195
telephone, 188–195, 199, 209
television, 170, 194
Telser, Lester, 36
*Territorial Imperative, The* (Ardrey), 147
Thayer, Lee, 11, 42, 43
theories, 70, 77
*Theory of the Leisure Class, The* (Veblen), 64, 142
*Theory of Moral Sentiments* (Smith), 4, 73, 76, 83, 114
thermodynamics, 102–105, 120 n. 32, 171, 224
threat, 170
throughput, 104
Thunder Bay (Ontario), 187
Tinder, Glen, 82, 83, 84 n. 6
Third World, 44–45
threat, 45, 170–171
threshold, 99, 119 n. 22
time's arrow, 98
Toffler, Alvin, 9, 79
Toronto, 193, 214
trade. *See* exchange
Trans Canada Telephone System. *See* Stentor Telecom Policy Inc
transaction costs, 33, 56, 77, 91–93, 118 n. 17
transnationals, 6, 112, 113, 201–204, 207, 221
transportation, 170
Troyer, W., 192
truth, 225, 226
TV Ontario, 211
typewriters, 170

uncertainty, 22, 24, 33–36, 39, 47 n. 5, 166

Underhill, Frank, 214
UNESCO, 18, 45, 207, 209 n. 5, 210 n. 5, 219
Union of Canadian Municipalities, 196
unions, 113, 205
uniqueness, 99
United States, 44, 113, 129, 208, 209 n. 4, 210 n. 5, 219
Unitel Communications Inc. ,188
University of Chicago, 143, 144, 159, 218
University of Manitoba, 212
user pay, 46, 202, 218, 219
utility. *See* preferences

valuation, 97, 115
value, 11, 14, 30, 32, 35, 65, 89, 99, 108, 114, 117 n. 17, 225
    exchange value 30, 47 n. 3, 48 n. 10, 98–100, 115
    intrinsic value, 47 n. 3, 48 n. 10, 99, 100, 115
    use value 47 n. 3
    *See also* prices
value added carriers, 191, 199
*Vancouver Sun,* 109, 121 n. 38
VCRs, 216
Veblen, Thorstein, 5, 21, 24, 40, 47 n. 5, 64–65, 67 n. 10, 75, 83, 126, 131, 135, 136, 141–158, 160, 168, 175–176
Vogel, Harold, 40, 109
volition. *See* freedom
voluntarism, 135, 211
von Bertalanffy, Ludwig, 57, 153, 221–222
von Weiszäcker, F., 11, 12, 41–42

Wade, Larry, 70
Wallace, Alfred Russel, 127, 134–137, 139 n. 12, 142, 153
Walras, Léon, 69, 127
*War of the Worlds,* 39, 67 n. 7
Washington, 193
WCAP, 193
WEAF, 193
wealth, 87, 88
*Wealth of Nations, The* (Smith), 4, 53, 66 n. 2, 69, 72, 73, 76, 78, 83, 114, 115, 138 n. 5

Weaver, W., 38, 47 n. 7
Webb, Sidney and Beatrice, 139 n. 10
Weber, Max, 51, 225
Webster, Frank, 43
Weizenbaum, Joseph, 80
Welles, H. G., 139 n. 10
Welles, Orson, 39, 40, 67 n. 7
Western Electric, 193
Western Union, 186, 187,188
Westinghouse, 192
White, Leslie, 79
Whitehead, Alfred North, 126
Wiener, Norbert, 11, 57, 101, 153, 215
Williams, Raymond, 60, 110, 195
Wilson, Kevin, 82, 204
Winch, Donald, 129
Winner, Langdon, 80, 181, 183, 196
Winnipeg, 185, 189

Winter, James, 121 n. 39
Wood, N., 12
workmanship, 147, 150–151
World Commission on Environment
    and Development (WCED, Brunt-
    land Commission), 46
World Trade Organization, 44, 87, 88,
    116 n.1, 116 n. 2, 116 n. 4, 207
world system. *See* globalization
World War I, 192, 193

XWA, 192, 193, 197 n. 14

Yale University, 154 n. 2
Young R. M., 129, 133